I0648591

Samuel Arthur Jones

Bibliography of Henry David Thoreau

With an Outline of His Life

Samuel Arthur Jones

Bibliography of Henry David Thoreau
With an Outline of His Life

ISBN/EAN: 9783743441910

Manufactured in Europe, USA, Canada, Australia, Japa

Cover: Foto ©Raphael Reischuk / pixelio.de

Manufactured and distributed by brebook publishing software
(www.brebook.com)

Samuel Arthur Jones

Bibliography of Henry David Thoreau

... "The bachelor of
thought and Nature."

BIBLIOGRAPHY
OF HENRY DAVID
THOREAU
WITH AN OUTLINE
OF HIS LIFE

COMPILED AND CHRONO-
LOGICALLY ARRANGED BY

SAMUEL ARTHUR JONES

ERRATA.

Page 32, third line from bottom. For "July 4–21" read "July 4. Published July 21."

Page 33, second line. For "July 4–27" read "July 4. Published July 27."

Page 33, twelfth line. For "vol. xxx" read "vol. iii."

Page 44, fifth line. For "edition princeps" read "editio princeps."

Page 54. Instead of the last entry, read

Familiar Letters of | Henry David Thoreau | Edited, with an Introduction and Notes | By | F. B. Sanborn | Cambridge | Printed at the Riverside Press | 1894.

Vol. XI of the series. Pp. v–xii, 1–483. Photogravure portrait after the Ricketson medallion. The original edition of the Letters contains only sixty-five; this gives one hundred and twenty-eight.

Page 69, first line. For "Forrester" read "Forester."

Contents

Chronology of Thoreau's Life
1817 — 1862

The life of a scholar seldom abounds with adventure. His fame is acquired in solitude, and the historian who only views him at a distance, must be content with a dry detail of actions by which he is scarce distinguished from the rest of Mankind.
GOLDSMITH.

1817. HENRY DAVID THOREAU was born in Concord, Massachusetts, on the twelfth of July.

1818. His parents moved to Chelmsford, and shortly afterward to Boston, where he first attended school.

1823. The family returned to Concord, where he was prepared for college. "I was fitted, or rather made unfit, for college at Concord Academy and elsewhere, mainly by myself with the coun-

2   9

tenance of Phineas Allen, Preceptor."
(Thoreau, Letter to the Class Secretary.)

1833. Entered Harvard University.
"'One branch more,' to use Mr. Quin-
cy's words, 'and you had been turned
by entirely. You have barely got in.'
However, 'A man's a man for a' that.'
I was in, and did not stop to ask how I
got there." (Letter to the Class Secretary.)

1834. Began keeping a diary. In
this year Emerson delivered his first lecture in Concord. "I believe I never
thanked you for your lectures, one and
all, which I heard formerly read here in
Concord. I *know* I never have. There
was some excellent reason each time
why I did not; but it will never be too
late. I have had that advantage, at
least, over you in my education."
(Thoreau, Letter to Emerson, 1848).

1835. Between college terms taught
school at Canton, near Boston, where he

boarded and also studied German with the Rev. Orestes A. Brownson.

1836. "Went to New York with father, peddling." His health had failed, and he was obliged to absent himself from college.

1837. Was graduated at Harvard, in August. Camped by Lincoln Pond, with Stearns Wheeler. Later, taught in the Concord Academy. "Notwithstanding what he himself says of his entrance to the college, and the impression one gets from some of his biographers, Thoreau maintained a very fair rank in his class, and at graduation took part in a conference with Charles Wyatt Rice and Henry Vose on the 'Commercial Spirit of Modern Times, Considered in its Influence on the Political, Moral, and Literary Character of a Nation.'" (Memorials of the Class of 1837 of Harvard University.) What he himself says: " Though bodily I have been a member of Harvard University, heart

11

and soul I have been far away among
the scenes of my boyhood. Those
hours that should have been devoted to
study have been spent in scouring the
woods and exploring the lakes and
streams of my native village. Immured
within the dark but classic walls of a
Stoughton or a Hollis, my spirit yearned
for the sympathy of my old and almost
forgotten friend, Nature." (Letter to the
Class Secretary.)

1838. Teaching in the Concord Academy. On the eleventh of April delivered his first lecture in Concord, on
Society. In December wrote a mem-
orable essay on Sound and Silence.

1839. He and his brother John made
the voyage on the Concord and Merrimack rivers.

1840. Teaching school in Concord,
with his brother John. Wrote his first
published prose paper, on Aulus Perseus
Flaccus. Became a contributor to the
Dial.

1841. Became an inmate of Emerson's house, where he resided for two years.

1842. In February his brother John died. In July Thoreau made a three days' excursion to Wachusett. Published his essay on The Natural History of Massachusetts, in the Dial. "By the middle of 1842 the Dial, which had never been prosperous from a pecuniary point of view, was in severe straights, and the editorship, having been resigned by Margaret Fuller, was undertaken by Emerson himself, in which work he was largely assisted by Thoreau."

1843. Left Concord to serve as tutor in the family of Emerson's brother, at Staten Island. Published his Walk to Wachusett. Translated The Seven Against Thebes.

1844. Returned to Concord, where he ever after resided.

1845. In March borrowed Mr. Alcott's axe, to build the shanty at Walden. "The owner of the axe, as he released his hold on it, said that it was the apple of his eye; but I returned it sharper than I received it. . . . By the middle of April, for I made no haste in my work, but rather made the most of it, my house was framed and ready for the raising. . . . At length, in the beginning of May, with the help of some of my acquaintances, rather to improve so good an occasion for neighborliness than from any necessity, I set up the frame of my house. . . . I began to occupy my house on the 4th of July. . . . My purpose in going to Walden was not to live cheaply, nor to live dearly there, but to transact some private business with the fewest obstacles."

1846. Living at Walden Pond. Wrote his essay on Carlyle. Arrested and put into Concord jail for refusing to pay taxes. "Declining to pay taxes, he went cheerfully to jail, and when his friend, Mr. Emerson, hastened to the

prison and said to him, with amaze-
ment, 'Henry, why are you here?' the
placid prisoner answered quietly, 'Why
are you *not* here?'" (George W. Curtis, in The Easy Chair.) "I have paid
no poll-tax for six years. I was put
into jail once on this account, for one
night; and, as I stood considering the
walls of solid stone, two or three feet
thick, the door of wood and iron, a foot
thick, and the iron grating which strained
the light, I could not help being struck
with the foolishness of that institution
which treated me as if I were mere flesh
and bones to be locked up. I wondered
that it should have concluded at length
that this was the best use it could put
me to, and had never thought to avail
itself of my services in some way. I
saw that, if there was a wall of stone
between me and my townsmen, there
was still a more difficult one to climb or
break through before they could get to
be as free as I was. I did not for a mo-
ment feel confined, and the walls seemed

to be a great waste of stone and mortar. I felt as if I alone of all my townsmen had paid my tax. They plainly did not know how to treat me, but behaved like persons who are underbred. In every threat and in every compliment there was a blunder; for they thought that my chief desire was to stand the other side that stone wall. I could not but smile to see how industriously they locked the door on my meditations, which followed them out again without let or hindrance, and *they* really were all that was dangerous. As they could not reach me, they had resolved to punish my body; just as boys, if they cannot come at some person against whom they have a spite, will abuse his dog. I saw that the State was half-witted, that it was as timid as a lone woman with her silver spoons, and that it did not know its friends from its foes, and I lost all my remaining respect for it." At the end of August Thoreau made his first visit to the Maine woods.

1847. In September left the shanty at Walden Pond to reside again at Emerson's while he was absent lecturing in England. In 1847, in answer to a circular which was issued at the time for the purpose of collecting facts in the lives of the class during the first decade of our experience in the world, he writes as follows: "Am not married. I don't know whether mine is a profession, or a trade, or what not. It is not yet learned, and in every instance has been practised before being studied. The mercantile part of it was begun here by myself alone. It is not one, but legion. I will give you some of the monster's heads. I am a Schoolmaster, a Private Tutor, a Surveyor, a Gardener, a Farmer, a Painter (I mean a House Painter), a Carpenter, a Mason, a Day-laborer, a Pencil-maker, a Glass-paper-maker, a Writer, and sometimes a Poetaster. If you will act the part of Iolas, and apply a hot iron to any of these heads, I shall be greatly obliged to you. My present employment is to answer such orders as may be expected from so general an advertisement as the above. That is, if I see fit, which is not always the case, for I have found out a way to live without what is commonly called employment, or industry attractive or otherwise. Indeed, my steadiest employment, if such it can be called, is to keep myself at the top of my condition, and ready for whatever may turn up in heaven or on earth. The last two or three years I have lived in Concord woods, alone, in a house built entirely by myself. P. S. I beg that the class will not consider me an object of charity, and if any of them are in want of any pecuniary assistance and will make known their case to me, I will engage to give them some advice of more worth than money." (Letter to the Class Secretary in 1847.)

1848. Still residing at Emerson's. "Lectures begin to multiply on my desk. I have one on Friendship which is new, and the materials of others. I read one last week to the Lyceum on The Rights and Duties of the Individual in Relation to Government, much to Mr. Alcott's satisfaction." (Letter to Emerson.)

1849. Published A Week on the Concord and Merrimack Rivers. In October made his first visit to Cape Cod. His essay on Resistance to Civil Government published in Æsthetic Papers. This was the lecture that had given Mr. Alcott such satisfaction.

1850. In June Thoreau made his second visit to Cape Cod. In July went to Fire Island to look for the body and effects of Margaret Fuller, Countess d'Ossoli. In September started from Concord with Ellery Channing for a week's sojourn in Canada.

1851. Residing in Concord, and lecturing. "I have been told by a man who when a boy heard him read a lecture, that the audience did not know what to make of him. They came out hardly knowing whether they had been sold or not. His coolness, his paradoxes, his strange and extreme gospel of nature, and evidently his indifference as to whether he pleased them or not, were not in the line of the popular lecturer." (John Burroughs.)

1852. At Concord, and still in the lecture field.

1853. Active in anti-slavery matters in Concord. Made his second visit to the Maine woods.

1854. Published Walden. Delivered his address on Slavery in Massachusetts during the Anti-Slavery Celebration at Framingham.

1855. Received "a nest of Indian books" from his English friend, Mr. Thomas Cholmondeley. "He busied himself in buying, and has caused to be forwarded to me by Chapman, a royal gift, in the shape of twenty-one distinct works (one in nine volumes,—forty-four in all), almost exclusively relating to Hindoo literature, and scarcely one of them is to be bought in America. I am familiar with many of them, and know how to prize them. I send you information of this as I might of the birth of a child."

1856. Visited Horace Greeley at Chappaqua. Made the acquaintance of Walt Whitman. "Since I have seen him, I find I am not disturbed by any brag or egoism in his book. He may turn out the least of a braggart of all, having a right to be confident. He is a great fellow." (Letter to Mr. Blake.)

1857. Introduced to Captain John Brown at Concord. "Travelled the length of Cape Cod on foot." In company with Edward Hoar, made his last visit to the Maine woods.

1858. Camped with Mr. Blake for two nights on the summit of Monadnock. Visited the White Mountains with Edward Hoar. Published Chesuncook.

1859. Death of his father, third of February. "Five minutes before 3 P. M., father died. I have touched a body which was flexible and warm, yet tenantless—warmed by what fire? I perceive that we partially die ourselves, through sympathy, at the death of each of our friends and relatives. Each such experience is an assault on our vital force. After long watching around the sick-bed of a friend, we too partially give up the ghost with him, and are the less to be identified with this state of things." (Journal, February 3, 1859.) On Sunday evening, the thirtieth of October, in the church vestry at Concord, delivered his Plea for Captain John Brown. Repeated it in Tremont Temple, Boston, on the first of September, and again on the third at Worcester, Massachusetts. "Before the

first friendly word had been spoken for
Captain John Brown, after his arrest, he
sent notices to most houses in Concord,
that he would speak in a public hall on
the condition and character of John
Brown on Sunday evening, and invited
all people to come. The Republican
Committee, the Abolitionist Committee,
sent him word that it was premature,
and not advisable. He replied, 'I did
not send to you for advice, but to an-
nounce that I am to speak.' The hall
was filled at an early hour by people of
all parties, and his earnest eulogy of the
hero was heard by all respectfully; by
many with a sympathy that surprised
themselves." (Emerson's Biographical
Sketch.) "This instant and unequivocal
endorsement of Brown by Thoreau, in
the face of the overwhelming public
opinion even among anti-slavery men,
throws a flood of light upon him. It is
the most significant act of his life. It
clinches him. It makes the colors fast."
(John Burroughs.) "Lowell says that

23

Thoreau 'looked with utter contempt on the august drama of destiny, of which his country was the scene, and on which the curtain had already risen'; but was it Thoreau, or Lowell, who found a voice when the curtain fell, after the first act of that drama, upon the scaffold of John Brown?" (T. W. Higginson.)

1860. Went with Ellery Channing for a five days' visit to Monadnock. This was the last excursion in which Thoreau camped out. In November he took the cold that was the beginning of his fatal illness.

1861. Made a journey to Minnesota with Horace Mann, Jr. Returned to Concord only to put his house in order. Spent his strength in revising his manuscripts, assisted by his sister Sophia.

1862. "You ask particularly after my health. I *suppose* that I have not many months to live; but, of course, I know nothing about it. I may add that I am enjoying existence as much as ever, and regret nothing." (Thoreau's last letter, dictated March 21.) Died at 8 A. M., the sixth of May, aged forty-four years, nine months, and twenty-four days.

Contributions to the Dial

1840–44

cord and Merrimack Rivers, first edition, p. 403 ; second edition, p. 405 ; Riverside edition, p. 506.

Volume II, No. 2.   October, 1841.

FRIENDSHIP, "Let such pure hate still under-prop," p. 204. Reprinted in A Week on the Concord and Merrimack Rivers, first edition, p. 300 ; second edition, p. 304 ; Riverside edition, p. 379 ; and in Letters to Various Persons, p. 214.

Volume III, No. 1.   July, 1842.

NATURAL HISTORY OF MASSACHUSETTS, p. 19. Reprinted in Excursions, p. 37 ; Riverside edition, volume ix, p. 127.

Volume III, No. 1.   July, 1842.

PRAYER, " Great God, I ask thee for no meaner pelf," p. 78. Reprinted in A Yankee in Canada, p. 120 ; Riverside edition, volume x, p. 363.

Volume III, No. 2.   October, 1842.

THE BLACK KNIGHT, "Be sure your fate," p. 180.   Reprinted in Riverside edition, volume x, p. 361.

Volume III, No. 2.   October, 1842.

THE INWARD MORNING, " Packed in my mind lie all the clothes," p. 198.   Reprinted in A Week on the Concord and Merrimack Rivers, first edition, p. 308 ; second edition, p. 311 ; Riverside edition, p. 388.

Volume III, No. 2. October, 1842.

FREE LOVE, "My love must be as free," p. 199. Reprinted in A Week on the Concord and Merrimack Rivers, first edition, p. 293; second edition, p. 296; Riverside edition, p. 369.

Volume III, No. 2. October, 1842.

THE POET'S DELAY, "In vain I see the morning rise," p. 200. Reprinted in A Week on the Concord and Merrimack Rivers, first edition, p. 362; second edition, p. 364; Riverside edition, p. 453.

Volume III, No. 2. October, 1842.

RUMORS FROM AN ÆOLIAN HARP, "There is a vale which none hath seen," p. 200. Reprinted in A Week on the Concord and Merrimack Rivers, first edition, p. 181; second edition, p. 185; Riverside edition, p. 229.

Volume III, No. 2. October, 1842.

THE MOON, "The full-orbed moon with unchanged ray," p. 222. Reprinted in Riverside edition, volume x, p. 362.

Volume III, No. 2. October, 1842.

TO THE MAIDEN IN THE EAST, "Low in the eastern sky," p. 222. Reprinted in A Week on the Concord and Merrimack Rivers, first edition, p. 51; second edition, p. 54; Riverside edition, p. 58.

Volume III, No. 2. October, 1842.

THE SUMMER RAIN, "My books I 'd fain cast off, I cannot read," p. 224. Reprinted in A Week on the Concord and Merrimack Rivers, first edition, p. 318; second edition, p. 320; Riverside edition, p. 397.

Volume III, No. 3. January, 1843.

THE LAWS OF MENU, selected by Thoreau, p. 331.

Volume III, No. 3. January, 1843.

THE PROMETHEUS BOUND, translation, p. 363. Reprinted in Riverside edition, volume x, p. 288.

Volume III, No. 4. April, 1843.

ANACREON, eleven poems translated, p. 484. Reprinted in A Week on the Concord and Merrimack Rivers, first edition, p. 238; second edition, p. 240; Riverside edition, p. 298.

Volume III, No. 4. April, 1843.

SAYINGS OF CONFUCIUS, selected, p. 493.

Volume III, No. 4. April, 1843.

TO A STRAY FOWL, "Poor bird! destined to lead thy life," p. 505. Reprinted in Riverside edition, volume x, p. 360.

Volume III, No. 4. April, 1843.

ORPHICS: I, Smoke; II, Haze, p. 505. Reprinted in Letters to Various Persons, pp. 225,

226. Smoke also reprinted in Walden, p. 271, and Haze in A Week on the Concord and Merrimack Rivers, first edition, p. 227; second edition, p. 229; Riverside edition, p. 284.

Volume III, No. 4.   April, 1843.

DARK AGES, p. 527. Reprinted in A Week on the Concord and Merrimack Rivers, first edition, p. 159; second edition, p. 164; Riverside edition, p. 200.

Volume III, No. 4.   April, 1843.

FROM CHAUCER, selected by Thoreau, p. 529.

Volume IV, No. 2.   October, 1843.

ETHNICAL SCRIPTURES, CHINESE FOUR BOOKS, selected by Thoreau, p. 205.

Volume IV, No. 2.   October, 1843.

A WINTER WALK, p. 211. Reprinted in Excursions, p. 109; Riverside edition, volume ix, p. 199.

Volume IV, No. 3.   January, 1844.

HOMER, OSSIAN, CHAUCER, p. 211. Reprinted in A Week on the Concord and Merrimack Rivers. Ossian, first edition, p. 362; second edition, p. 364; Riverside edition, p. 453. Chaucer, first edition, p. 386; second edition, p. 387; Riverside edition, p. 483.

Volume IV, No. 3.   January, 1844.

PINDAR, note and translations, p. 379. Reprinted in Riverside edition, volume x, p. 337.

Volume IV, No. 3. January, 1844.

THE PREACHING OF BUDDHA, selections, p. 391.

Volume IV, No. 3. January, 1844.

ETHNICAL SCRIPTURES, HERMES TRISMEGISTUS, selected, p. 402.

Volume IV, No. 4. April, 1844.

HERALD OF FREEDOM, p. 507. Reprinted in A Yankee in Canada, p. 206; Riverside edition, volume x, p. 70.

Volume IV, No. 4. April, 1844.

FRAGMENTS OF PINDAR, p. 513. Reprinted in Riverside edition, volume x, p. 337.

CONTRIBUTIONS TO OTHER MAGAZINES, 1843–1862

The Boston Miscellany. 1843.

A WALK TO WACHUSETT, vol. iii, p. 31. Reprinted in Excursions, p. 73; Riverside edition, vol. ix, p. 163.

The Democratic Review. 1843.

THE LANDLORD, vol. xiii, p. 427 (October). Reprinted in Excursions, p. 97; Riverside edition, vol. ix, p. 187.

PARADISE (TO BE) REGAINED, vol. xiii, p. 451 (November). Reprinted in A Yankee in Canada, p. 182; Riverside edition, vol. x, p. 38.

The Liberator. 1845–60.

WENDELL PHILLIPS BEFORE THE CONCORD LYCEUM, March 28, 1845. Reprinted in A Yankee in Canada, p. 274; Riverside edition, vol. x, p. 76.

SLAVERY IN MASSACHUSETTS. An address delivered at the Anti-Slavery Celebration at Framingham, Mass., July 4–21, 1854. Reprinted in A Yankee in Canada, p. 97; Riverside edition, vol. x, p. 171.

The Last Days of John Brown. Read at
North Elba, N. Y., July 4–27, 1860. Reprinted in
A Yankee in Canada, p. 278; Riverside edition,
vol. x, p. 237.

Graham's Magazine. 1845.

Thomas Carlyle and his Works, vol. xxx,
p. 145 (March). Thomas Carlyle and his
Works, vol. xxx, p. 238 (April). Reprinted in A
Yankee in Canada, p. 211; Riverside edition, vol.
x, p. 81.

The Union Magazine. 1845.

Ktaadn and the Maine Woods, vol. xxx.
I. The Wilds of the Penobscot, p. 29 (January).
II. Life in the Wilderness, p. 73 (February). III.
Boating on the Lakes, p. 132 (March). IV. The
Ascent of Ktaadn, p. 177 (April). V. The Re-
turn Journey, p. 216 (May). Reprinted in The
Maine Woods, pp. 1 to 84; Riverside edition,
pp. 1 to 111.

Æsthetic Papers. 1849.

Resistance to Civil Government, p. 189.
Reprinted in A Yankee in Canada, p. 123; Riverside edition, vol. x, p. 131.

Putnam's Magazine. 1853–55.

Excursion to Canada, vol. i, 1853. I. Concord to Montreal, p. 54 (January). II. Quebec
and Montmorenci, p. 179 (February). III. St.

Anne, p. 321 (March). Reprinted in A Yankee in Canada, p. 3 ; Riverside edition, vol. ix, p. 9.

CAPE COD, vol. v, 1855. I. The Shipwreck, p. 632 (June). II. The Plains of Nanset, vol. 5, p. 59 (July). III. The Beach, vol. v, p. 157 (August). Reprinted in Cape Cod, p. 9; Riverside edition, vol. iv, p. 1.

The New York Tribune. 1860.

THE SUCCESSION OF FOREST TREES (read before the Middlesex Agricultural Society, Concord, September, 1860), October 6. Reprinted in Excursions, p. 135 ; Riverside edition, vol. ix, p. 225.

Echoes of Harper's Ferry.
Boston : Thayer & Eldridge, 1860.

A PLEA FOR CAPTAIN JOHN BROWN (read to the citizens of Concord, Mass., Sunday evening, October 30, 1859), pp. 16 to 42. Reprinted in A Yankee in Canada, p. 152; Riverside edition, vol. x, p. 197.

REMARKS AT CONCORD ON THE DAY OF THE EXECUTION OF JOHN BROWN (December 2, 1860), pp. 439 to 445. Reprinted in Riverside edition, vol. x, p. 237.

The Atlantic Monthly. 1858–93.

CHESUNCOOK, vol. ii (June, July, August, 1858). I, p. 1 ; II, p. 224; III, p. 305. Reprinted in The Maine Woods, p. 85 ; Riverside edition, p. 112.

WALKING, vol. ix, p. 657 (June, 1862). Reprinted in Excursions, p. 161; Riverside edition, vol. ix, p. 251.

AUTUMNAL TINTS, vol. x, p. 385 (October, 1862). Reprinted in Excursions, p. 215; Riverside edition, vol. ix, p. 305.

WILD APPLES, vol. x, p. 513 (November, 1862). Reprinted in Excursions, p. 266; Riverside edition, vol. ix, p. 356.

LIFE WITHOUT PRINCIPLE, vol. xii, p. 484 (October, 1863). Reprinted in A Yankee in Canada, p. 248; Riverside edition, vol. ix, p. 253.

NIGHT AND MOONLIGHT, vol. xii, p. 579 (November, 1863). Reprinted in Excursions, p. 307; Riverside edition, vol. ix, p. 397.

THE WELLFLEET OYSTERMAN, vol. xiv, p. 470 (October, 1864). Reprinted in Cape Cod, p. 72; Riverside edition, p. 92.

THE HIGHLAND LIGHT, vol. xiv, p. 649 (December, 1864). Reprinted in Cape Cod, p. 138; Riverside edition, p. 179.

APRIL DAYS, vol. xli, p. 445 (April, 1878). Reprinted in Riverside edition, vol. v, pp. 294, 322.

MAY DAYS, vol. xli, p. 567 (May, 1878). Reprinted in Riverside edition, vol. ix, p. 410.

DAYS IN JUNE, vol. xli, p. 711 (June, 1878). Reprinted in Riverside edition, vol. v.

Winter Days, vol. lv, p. 79 (January, 1885). Reprinted in Riverside edition, vol. viii.

The Emerson-Thoreau Correspondence, vol. lxix, p. 577 (May, 1892).

The Emerson-Thoreau Correspondence, vol. lxix, p. 736 (June, 1892).

Thoreau and his English Friend, Thomas Cholmondeley, vol. lxxii, p. 741 (December, 1893).

The Boston Commonwealth. 1863.

Inspiration, vol. i, No. 42 (June 19).

The Funeral Bell, vol. i, No. 44 (July 3).

Travelling: Greece, vol. i, No. 47 (July 24).

The Departure, vol. i, No. 52 (August 28).

The Fall of the Leaf, vol. ii, No. 58 (October 9).

Independence, vol. ii, No. 61 (October 30).

The Soul's Season, vol. ii, No. 62 (November 6).

[All these contributions to the Commonwealth are poems, and of them only Inspiration has been republished. It was included among the nine poems issued by Emerson in the posthumous volume of Letters, and as there given has only seven stanzas. The version in the Commonwealth consists of twenty-one stanzas.]

A Week | on the | Concord and Merrimack Rivers. | By | Henry D. Thoreau. | Boston and Cambridge: | James Munroe & Company. | New York: George Putnam. Philadelphia: Lindsay | and Blakiston. London: John Chapman. | 1849.

12°, pp. 1–413. Title-page and succeeding two leaves without pagination. Pp. iii, iv, v, poetry; p. vi, blank. Concord River, pp. 7–14; Saturday, pp. 15–44; Sunday, pp. 45–120; Monday, pp. 121–185; Tuesday, pp. 187–246; Wednesday, pp. 247–311; Thursday, pp. 313–350; Friday, pp. 351–413. Reverse of p. 413 is blank; the succeeding page announces: "Will soon be published, Walden, or Life in the Woods. By Henry D. Thoreau."

One thousand copies were printed at the author's risk. Of these, seventy-five were given away, two hundred and nineteen were sold, and the remaining seven hundred and six were returned to Thoreau on October, 28, 1853. In the face of such a reception, Walden was published in the succeeding year.

A Week | on the Concord and Mer-
rimack Rivers. | By | Henry D. Tho-
reau. | Author of "Walden." | Bos-
ton: | Ticknor and Fields. | 1862.

12°, pp. 1—413. Excepting the title-page,
this edition is exactly similar to the first. The ex-
planation of this was first given by a writer in The
Inlander, a monthly published by the undergradu-
ates of the University of Michigan. The article
is republished here in order to demonstrate that
bibliography is not necessarily an arid pursuit.

An Afternoon in the University Library.

"I am the 'most thumbed book' in this library,
as Willis said to Walter Savage Landor about the
Imaginary Conversations."

I looked around in surprise, for I was certain of
being the only person in the alcoves that sultry
afternoon.

"Nor has any book a more romantic history."

I jumped to my feet and sought the speaker.

"The manuscript of me lay neglected in the
desks of caitiff publishers; it was despised and rejected when read by their 'tasters'; dealt out at
last piecemeal in a dog's meat-tart of a journal;
pirated into a book by a Yankee admirer—the
more 's the wonder; and two years later printed
at home on the 'half profits' plan, which I com-

pute generally to mean equal partition of the oyster *shells* and a net result of *zero*."

> That trick i' the voice I do well remember;
> Is 't not the King?

Shakespeare's lines leapt to my lips, and I involuntarily added, "Carlyle!" Was ever the like? Right by my side, on an alcove shelf, was a well-worn copy of Sartor Resartus, and, as I am a living man, talking.

"You may be the 'most thumbed book' in this library. What of that? More people eat potatoes than *pâtés de foie gras*. I am not 'thumbed.' I find audience fit though few. I claim, however, a more romantic history than yours. I am one of a thousand copies. The first of us to leave the publisher's shop was sent as a present to one of the gentlest souls that ever brake the bread of friendship. It went to Worcester, Massachusetts. After some time, seventy-four more of us were given away. In the course of four years two hundred and nineteen of us were slowly sold over the counter. We were often looked at, and as often put down again with a disgusted 'Humph!' At the beginning of our third year of existence the remaining seven hundred and six of us were piled up in the publisher's cellar. We were tied up in close packages of fifty, and had we not been immortal we had smothered. After two weary years in that abode, we were taken forth and sent by express to Concord, Massachusetts. There we were received by a rustic-looking man who had the serenest face I ever saw, and he handled us with more tenderness than any that had yet touched us. On his own back he carried us, parcel after parcel, up to the garret of his father's house ; and when he had piled us compactly he wiped the sweat from his brow, and then surveyed us with a look of quiet cheerfulness. I happened to be at the top corner of the package I was in, and, the paper having been torn during our journey, I could easily look over his shoulder when, all at once, he sat down at a plain pine desk and wrote in a book:

" ' For a year or two past my publisher, falsely so called, has been writing from time to time to ask what disposition should be made of the copies of A Week on the Concord and Merrimack Rivers still on hand, and at last suggesting that he had use for the room they occupied in his cellar. So I had them all sent to me here, and they have arrived to-day by express, filling the man's wagon, — seven hundred and six copies out of an edition of one thousand, which I bought of Munroe four years ago and have ever since been paying for, and have not quite paid for yet. The wares are sent to me at last, and I have an opportunity to examine my purchase. They are something more substantial than fame, as my back knows, which has borne them up two flights of stairs to a place quite similar to that to which they trace their origin.

Of the remaining two hundred ninety and odd, seventy-five were given away, the rest sold. I now have a library of nearly nine hundred volumes, over seven hundred of which I wrote myself. Is it not well that the author should behold the fruits of his labors? My works are piled up in my chamber half as high as my head—my *opera omnia*. This is authorship. These are the work of my brain. There was just one piece of good luck in the venture. The unbound copies were tied up by the printer four years ago in stout paper wrappers, and inscribed, "H. D. Thoreau, Concord River. 50 cops." So Munroe had only to cross out "River" and write "Mass.," and deliver them to the expressman at once. I can see now what I write for, the result of my labors. Nevertheless, in spite of this result, sitting beside the inert mass of my works, I take up my pen to-night to record what thought or experience I have had with as much satisfaction as ever. Indeed, I believe that the result is more inspiring and better for me than if a thousand had bought my wares. It affects my privacy less and leaves me freer.' [1]

"Day after day, for nine long years, we lay in that garret, and night after night I saw that man writing in his book at the desk. But of late he coughed a great deal, and night by night I saw that he wrote less. I often caught a look of deep longing in his eyes when he peered out of the garret win-

1 Thoreau's Journal, October 28, 1853.

dow on the distant fields; but he did not seem sad, and I never heard from him a single sigh nor one repining word. One day a solemn hymn floated through the window on the wings of a May breeze to our resting-place, and then it ceased; and nevermore did I see that serene man writing at the pine desk. Some months later we were transported from that garret to the bindery of Ticknor & Fields, and thence to the Old Corner Bookstore, each of us having on a new jacket and wearing a new title-page. The latter purported that each of us was published by Ticknor & Fields, Boston, 1862, when the actual truth is that we were at that date just fourteen years old—no sucklings, I assure you. But I laughed; for, you see, the binder had not bethought him to tear out a back leaf which announced to the reader that 'Walden, or Life in the Woods, will soon be published.' Why, bless you, that identical book had been published by Ticknor & Fields nine years before! I am an editio princeps, despite my lying title-page; I was born in my author's brain, and I was borne on his back when I, too, was 'despised and rejected.'"

"An' do ye say that when ye cam' flouted back into yon garret your maker received ye as cheerily an' bravely as ye tell?"

"Even as I said," was the reply.

"Then I tak' back every vaporin' word o' mine, and will sit at your feet as long as books are read."

· · · · · ·

" I beg your pardon, Mr. Philliber, but it's time to close the library." It was the good librarian, and as he caught me napping when I should have been reading I told him what I had dreamed.

To be sure, the dream was a book-lover's fantasy, but it was also the simple truth. Every copy of the 1862 edition of Thoreau's Week is a first edition. The seven hundred and five copies of the unbound sheets — Thoreau had sold one copy — were bought from the family by James T. Fields and sold with the new title-page within five years from the date of Thoreau's death. Then a new edition, from fresh type, was issued, the plates of which did service until the publishing of the Riverside edition in 1893.

A | Week | on the | Concord and Merrimack Rivers. | By Henry D. Thoreau, | Author of " Walden," etc. | New and Revised Edition. | Boston: | Ticknor and Fields. | 1867.

16°, pp. 1–415. Bastard title, title-page, and two succeeding leaves without pagination. Pp. v, vi, vii, viii, poetry. The citation from Ovid, and its translation on p. viii, appear for the first time in this edition.

This edition introduces two errors into the text that have ever since been reproduced. Thoreau wrote, "There is need of a physician who shall minister to both soul and body at once, that is to man. Now he falls between two stools." (Edition princeps, p. 271.) In this edition, p. 273, the text reads, "Now he falls between two souls." In the original edition, p. 412, Thoreau has, "It were vain for me to endeavor to interpret the Silence." In this edition, p. 414, it is printed, "It were vain for me to endeavor to interrupt the Silence."

A Week on the Concord and Merrimac Rivers, By Henry Thoreau: with A Prefaratory Note by Will. H. Dircks. London: Walter Scott, 24 Warwick Lane. [1889.]

The Camelot Series. This is the first English edition, and it reproduces the two errors of the American edition of 1867.

A Week on the Concord | and Merrimack Rivers | by Henry David Thoreau | Cambridge | Printed at the Riverside Press | 1894 [1893].

Two editions were published, a large paper 8°, 150 copies, and the Riverside edition, 12°; pp.

i–xvii, 1–531. The Rowse portrait is reproduced, and the value of this edition is greatly enhanced by a publisher's note, table of contents, a table of the quotations made by Thoreau in the course of the volume, and a comprehensive index. Vol. I of the series. This volume was set up from a copy of the edition of 1867, and it therefore perpetuates the before-mentioned typographical errors on pp. 339, 517.

Walden; | or, | Life in the Woods. | By Henry D. Thoreau, | Author of " A Week on the Concord and Merrimack Rivers." | [Wood-engraving of the shanty at Walden Pond.] | [Motto from p. 92 of the book.] | Boston : | Ticknor and Fields. | M DCCC LIV.

12°, pp. 1–357. First two leaves without pagination; p. 3, contents; p. 4, blank; map of Walden Pond facing p. 307. The original plates of this edition were in use until the appearance of the Riverside edition of 1894 [1893].

Walden | By | Henry D. Thoreau | Author of | " A Week on the Concord and Merrimack Rivers." | In Two Volumes. | [Motto.] | Boston and New

York | Houghton, Mifflin and Company | The Riverside Press, Cambridge | 1889.

The Riverside Aldine Series. Neither the engraving of the shanty nor the plan of Walden Pond is reproduced.

Walden. By Henry David Thoreau. With an Introductory Note by Will Dircks. London: Walter Scott, 24 Warwick Lane. 1888.

The Camelot Series. This is the first English edition; it lacks the engravings of the original issue.

Walden | or, | Life in the Woods | by | Henry D. Thoreau | [Motto.] | Cambridge | Printed at the Riverside Press | 1894 [1893].

Vol. II of the series. Two editions published, a large paper and the Riverside; pp. i–viii, 1–522. Has table of contents, introductory note, and index. The plan of Walden Pond and the engraving of the shanty are omitted.

Excursions. | By Henry D. Thoreau, | Author of "Walden," and "A Week on the Concord and | Merrimack Rivers." | Boston : | Ticknor and Fields. | 1863.

12°, pp. 1–319. Steel engraving of the crayon by Rowse. This is the first engraved portrait of Thoreau. The volume contains Emerson's Biographical Sketch, and was edited jointly by him and Sophia Thoreau. There is no later edition that follows this in arrangement and contents.

Excursions | by | Henry David Thoreau | Cambridge | Printed at the Riverside Press | 1894 [1893].

Vol. IX of the series. Two editions published ; pp. i–ix, 1–472. Has table of contents, introductory note, and index. This volume differs from the original of the same name by containing A Yankee in Canada, May Days, and Days in June.

The Maine Woods | By Henry D. Thoreau, | Author of " A Week on the Concord and Merrimack Rivers," | "Walden," "Excursions," etc., etc. | Boston : | Ticknor and Fields. | 1864.

12°, pp. 1–328. Title-page and two succeeding leaves without pagination. Edited jointly by Sophia Thoreau and William Ellery Channing.

The Maine Woods | by | Henry D. Thoreau | Cambridge | Printed at the Riverside Press | 1894 [1893].

Vol. III of the series. Two editions published; pp. i–ix, 1–442. Has table of contents, intro-ɾ ductory note, and index.

Cape Cod. | By Henry D. Thoreau, | Author of " A Week on the Concord and Merrimack Rivers," | " Walden," "Excursions," " The Maine Woods," ɾ etc., etc. | [Motto.] | Boston: Ticknor and Fields. | 1865 [1864].

12°, pp. 1–252. Title-page and succeeding leaf without pagination. Edited jointly by Sophia Thoreau and William Ellery Channing.

Cape Cod | by | Henry David Thoreau | [Motto.] | Cambridge | Printed at the Riverside Press | 1894 [1893].

Vol. IV of the series. Two editions published; pp. 1–336. Title-page and two succeeding leaves without pagination. Has introductory note, table of contents, and index.

Letters | to Various Persons. | By
Henry D. Thoreau, | Author of "A
Week on the Concord and Merrimack
Rivers," | "Walden," etc., etc. | Bos-
ton: | Ticknor and Fields. | 1865.

12°, pp. 1–229. Title-page and two succeeding leaves without pagination. Editor's notice.
Pp. 211–229 contain nine poems selected by Emerson. Edited by R. W. Emerson. This volume
has not been republished in the Riverside edition.

Essays and other Writings of Henry
Thoreau: Edited, with a Prefatory Note,
by Will H. Dircks. London: Walter
Scott, 24 Warwick Lane, Paternoster
Row. n. d. [1891.]

The Camelot Series. This volume contains a
selection from the Letters, and the nine poems previously published by Emerson.

A | Yankee in Canada, | with | Anti-
Slavery and Reform | Papers. | By |
Henry D. Thoreau, | Author of "A
Week on the Concord and Merrimack
Rivers," | "Walden," "Cape Cod,"

etc., etc. | Boston : Ticknor and Fields.
| 1866.

12°, pp. 1–286. Title-page and two succeeding
leaves without pagination. The article Prayers,
on p. 116, is ascribed to Thoreau by mistake, only
the verses, "Great God, I ask thee for no meaner
pelf," being his. Edited jointly by Sophia Thoreau and William Ellery Channing. No other edition is like this in arrangement and contents.

Early Spring in Massachusetts. | From
the Journal of | Henry D. Thoreau, |
Author of " A Week on the Concord
and Merrimack Rivers," | "Walden,"
etc. | [Motto.] | Boston : | Houghton,
Mifflin and Company. | The Riverside
Press, Cambridge. 1881.

12°, pp. i–vii, 1–318. Introductory. Edited
by H. G. O. Blake, Thoreau's literary executor
after the death of Sophia Thoreau. A revised
and corrected edition with a much-needed appen-
dix was published by the copyright holders in 1890.

Early Spring in Massachusetts | From
the Journal of | Henry David Tho-
reau | Edited by | H. G. O. Blake |

[Motto.] | Cambridge | Printed at the Riverside Press | 1894 [1893].

Vol. V of the series. Two editions published; pp. i–ix, 1–354. Reproduction, in photogravure, of Moxham's daguerreotype of Thoreau. Has editor's introductory note, note on the portrait, and index. This volume contains April Days, first published in the Atlantic Monthly, and inadvertently omitted from the edition of 1881.

Summer: From the Journal | of Henry D. Thoreau | Edited by H. G. O. Blake | [Motto.] | Boston : | Houghton, Mifflin and Company | The Riverside Press, Cambridge | 1884.

12°, pp. i–v, 1–382. Has frontispiece, map of the town of Concord, editor's introductory note, and index.

Summer | From the Journal of Henry David Thoreau | Edited by | H. G. O. Blake | [Motto.] | Cambridge | Printed at the Riverside Press | 1894 [1893].

Vol. VI of the series. Two editions published; pp. i–vii, 1–382. Has frontispiece, map of town of Concord, editor's introductory note, and index.

Winter: From the Journal | of Henry D. Thoreau | Edited by H. G. O. Blake | [Motto.] | Boston and New York | Houghton, Mifflin and Company | The Riverside Press, Cambridge | 1888.

12°, pp. i–vi, 1–439. Has editor's introductory note and index.

Winter | From the Journal of | Henry David Thoreau | Edited by | H. G. O. Blake | [Motto.] | Cambridge | Printed at the Riverside Press | 1894 [1893].

Vol. VIII of the series. Two editions published; pp. i–vii, 1–439. Has editor's introductory note and index.

Autumn: From the Journal | of Henry D. Thoreau | Edited by H. G. O. Blake | [Two mottos.] | Boston and New York | Houghton, Mifflin and Company | The Riverside Press, Cambridge | 1892.

12°, pp. i–vi, 1–470. Has editor's introductory note and index.

Autumn | From the Journal of | Henry David Thoreau | Edited by H. G. O. Blake | [Two mottos.] | Cambridge | Printed at the Riverside Press | 1894 [1893].

Vol. VII of the series. Two editions; pp. i–viii, 1–470. Has editor's introductory note and index.

Miscellanies | By | Henry David Thoreau | With a Biographical Sketch | By Ralph Waldo Emerson | and a General Index | to the Writings | Cambridge | Printed at the Riverside Press | 1894 [1893].

Vol. X of the series. Two editions published; pp. i–xi, 429. Steel engraving of the Dunshee ambrotype. Has table of contents, publisher's introductory note, and general index. In this volume are republished Thoreau's translation of Prometheus Bound, his translations from Pindar, and several poems from The Dial. The initial article is a fragmentary essay by Thoreau previously published only in the Concord Lectures on Philosophy for 1882. Here also is the transposed Biographical Sketch by Emerson, and all of the earlier volume, A Yankee in Canada, from p. 97 to the end. The arrangement is not the same..

Anti-Slavery and Reform Papers by
Henry D. Thoreau Selected and Edited
by H. S. Salt. London: Swan Sonnenschein & Co., Paternoster Square. 1890.

Contents: An introductory note by the editor;
Civil Disobedience; A Plea for Captain John
Brown; The Last Days of John Brown; Paradise
(to be) Regained; Life without Principle.

Essays and other Writings of Henry
Thoreau : Edited, with a Prefatory Note,
by Will H. Dircks. London: Walter
Scott, 24, Warwick Lane, Paternoster
Row. n. d.

Contents: Walking; A Winter Walk; Night
and Moonlight; The Landlord; Life without
Principle; Civil Disobedience; A Plea for Captain John Brown; The Last Days of John Brown;
Love, Chastity and Sensuality; Thomas Carlyle
and his Works; Letters; Poems.

Familiar Letters of Henry David
Thoreau. Edited with an Introduction
and Notes by F. B. Sanborn. The Riverside Press, Cambridge, 1894.

Vol. XI of the series. Pp. v–xii, 1–483.

The Order of Publication, Contents, and Arrangement of the Two Editions.

Original Edition.

1849. A Week on the Concord and Merrimack Rivers.

1854. Walden, or Life in the Woods.

1863. Excursions. Biographical Sketch; Natural History of Massachusetts; A Walk to Wachusett; The Landlord; A Winter Walk; The Succession of Forest Trees; Walking; Autumnal Tints; Wild Apples; Night and Moonlight.

1864. The Maine Woods.

1865. Cape Cod.

1865. Letters to Various Persons.

1866. A Yankee in Canada, with Anti-Slavery and Reform Papers. A Yankee in Canada; Slavery in Massachusetts; Prayers; Civil Disobedience; A Plea for Captain

John Brown; Paradise (to be) Regained;
Herald of Freedom; Thomas Carlyle and
his Works; Life without Principle; Wendell Phillips before the Concord Lyceum;
The Last Days of John Brown.

The Riverside Edition, 1894.

Vol. I. A WEEK ON THE CONCORD AND MERRI-
MACK RIVERS.

Vol. II. WALDEN, OR LIFE IN THE WOODS.

Vol. III. THE MAINE WOODS.

Vol. IV. CAPE COD.

Vol. V. EARLY SPRING IN MASSACHUSETTS.

Vol. VI. SUMMER.

Vol. VII. AUTUMN.

Vol. VIII. WINTER.

Vol. IX. EXCURSIONS. A Yankee in Canada;
Natural History of Massachusetts; A
Walk to Wachusett; The Landlord; A
Winter Walk; The Succession of Forest
Trees; Walking; Autumnal Tints; Wild
Apples; Night and Moonlight; May
Days; Days and Nights in Concord.

Vol. X. MISCELLANIES. Biographical Sketch; The
Service: Qualities of the Recruit; Paradise (to be) Regained; Herald of Freedom; Wendell Phillips before the Concord Lyceum; Thomas Carlyle and his

Works; Civil Disobedience; Slavery in Massachusetts; A Plea for Captain John Brown; The Last Days of John Brown; After the Death of John Brown; Life without Principle; The Prometheus Bound of Æschylus; Translations from Pindar; Poems: Inspiration, Pilgrims, To a Stray Fowl, The Black Knight, The Moon, Omnipresence, Inspiration, Prayer, Mission, Delay.

Vol. XI. FAMILIAR LETTERS.

Biographical
1862-90

1862

Biographical Sketch. By Ralph Waldo Emerson. Originally read at Thoreau's funeral. Enlarged, and published in the Atlantic Monthly, vol. x, p. 239. Republished in Excursions, p. 7; Riverside edition, vol. x, p. 1. Portrait, after Rowse's crayon of 1854, in each of these editions.

1873

Thoreau: The Poet-Naturalist. With memorial verses. By William Ellery Channing. Boston: Roberts Brothers. Originally published in the Boston Commonwealth, vol. ii, 18–63. This volume contains much of Thoreau's Journal that has not been published elsewhere.

1877

Thoreau: His Life and Aims. A Study. By H. A. Page [Dr. A. H. Japp]. Boston: James H. Osgood & Company. Woodcut portrait after Rowse.

1878

THOREAU: HIS LIFE AND AIMS. The English, and the original, edition. London: Chatto and Windus. Woodcut portrait after Rowse.

1882

HENRY D. THOREAU. By F. B. Sanborn. American Men of Letters Series. Boston: Houghton, Mifflin and Company. Steel engraving of the ambrotype taken for Mr. D. Ricketson by Dunshee, at New Bedford, Mass., 1861.

HENRY D. THOREAU. By F. B. Sanborn. London: Sampson, Low, Marston, Searle & Rivington.

1890

THE LIFE OF HENRY DAVID THOREAU. By H. S. Salt. London: Richard Bentley & Son. Portrait after the Rowse crayon.

59

ANA
1847-1893

1847

WILLIAM ELLERY CHANNING.   Poems, Second Series, p. 157. Boston: James Munroe and Company.

1848

JAMES RUSSELL LOWELL.   A Fable for Critics, p. 32.   [New York:] G. P. Putnam.

1849

WILLIAM ELLERY CHANNING.   The Woodman, and other Poems, Index. Boston: James Munroe and Company.

1853

GEORGE WILLIAM CURTIS. The Homes of American Authors, pp. 247-250. New York: G. P. Putnam & Co.

1855

E. A. and G. L. DUYCKINCK.   Cyclopedia of American Literature, vol. ii, p. 653.   New York: Charles Scribner.

1858

WILLIAM ELLERY CHANNING. Near Home, pp. 3–6, 30–35, 52. Boston: James Munroe and Company.

1863

RALPH WALDO EMERSON. Thoreau's Excursions, p. 7. Boston : Ticknor and Fields.

1866

W. R. ALGER. The Solitudes of Nature and of Man, p. 329. Boston: Roberts Brothers.

1868

NATHANIEL HAWTHORNE. Passages from the American Note-Books, vol. ii, pp. 96–99. Boston : Ticknor and Fields.

1869

DANIEL RICKETSON. The Autumn Sheaf: A Collection of Miscellaneous Verses, pp. 198, 199, 211. Published by the Author, New Bedford, Mass.

1870

R. W. GRISWOLD. Prose Writers of America, p. 657. Philadelphia: Porter & Coates. n. d.

1871

WILLIAM ELLERY CHANNING. The Wanderer, pp. 25–37, 61–77. Boston: James R. Osgood & Co.

JAMES RUSSELL LOWELL. My Study Windows, p. 193. Boston: James R. Osgood & Co

S. A. Allibone. Critical Dictionary of English Literature, vol. iii, p. 2406. Philadelphia: J. B. Lippincott Company.

1872
Wilson Flagg. The Woods and By-Ways of New England, p. 392. Boston: James R. Osgood & Co.

1873
Amos Bronson Alcott. Concord Days, pp. 11, 259. Boston: Roberts Brothers.

1878
F. B. Sanborn. Memoirs of John Brown, pp. 45, 49. Concord, Mass.

1879
P. C. Bliss. Johnson's Encyclopedia, p. 842. New York: A. J. Johnson & Co.

1880
Thomas Wentworth Higginson. Short Studies of American Authors, p. 23. Boston: Lee and Shepard.

James T. Fields. Papyrus Leaves, p. 29. New York: R. Worthington.

Henry James, Jr. Hawthorne (American Men of Letters), p. 93. New York: Harper and Brothers.

Horace E. Scudder. American Prose, p. 296. Boston: Houghton, Mifflin and Company.

1881

GEORGE W. COOKE. Ralph Waldo Emerson: His Life, Writings, and Philosophy. Index. Boston: James R. Osgood & Co.

WILSON FLAGG. Halcyon Days, p. 164. Boston: Estes and Lauriat.

JUSTIN WINSOR. Memorial History of Boston, vol. iii, p. 648. Boston: James R. Osgood & Co.

1882

MONCURE D. CONWAY. Emerson at Home and Abroad, p. 279. Boston: James R. Osgood & Co.

AMOS BRONSON ALCOTT. Sonnets and Canzonets. Boston: Roberts Brothers.

GEORGE STEWART, JR. Transactions of the Literary and Historical Society of Quebec, p. 121. Quebec.

PROF. JOHN NICHOL. American Literature: An Historical Sketch, p. 213. Edinburgh: Adam and Charles Black.

JOHN BURROUGHS. Essays from the Critic, p. 9. Boston: James R. Osgood & Co.

F. B. SANBORN. Concord Lectures on Philosophy, p. 67. Cambridge: Moses King.

F. B. SANBORN. Essays from the Critic, p. 71. Boston: James R. Osgood & Co.

1884

JULIAN HAWTHORNE. Nathaniel Hawthorne and his Wife: A Biography. Index. Boston: James R. Osgood & Co.

1885

F. B. SANBORN. Life and Letters of John Brown. Index. Boston: Roberts Brothers.

OLIVER WENDELL HOLMES. Ralph Waldo Emerson (American Men of Letters). Index. Boston: Houghton, Mifflin and Company.

1886

ROBERT LOUIS STEVENSON. Familiar Studies of Men and Books, p. 129. London: Chatto and Windus.

W. H. DIRCKS. Walden. With an Introductory Note, p. vii. The Camelot Series. London: Walter Scott.

RICHARD GARNETT. My Study Windows. With an Introduction, p. xv. The Camelot Series. London: Walter Scott.

1887

HENRY WILLIAMS. Memorials of the Class of 1837 of Harvard University, p. 37. Printed for the Class. Boston: Geo. H. Ellis.

DAVID GREEN HASKINS. Ralph Waldo Emerson: His Maternal Ancestors, pp. 119, 122. Boston: Cupples, Upham & Co.

E. P. Whipple. Recollections of Eminent Men. p. 134. Boston: Ticknor and Co.

Amanda B. Harris. American Literature for Young Folks, p. 163. Boston: D. Lothrop & Co.

Charles F. Richardson. American Literature, vol. i. Index. New York: G. P. Putnam's Sons.

E. P. Whipple. American Literature, and other Papers, p. 111. Boston: Ticknor & Co.

Prof. H. A. Seers. An Outline Sketch of American Literature, p. 143. New York: Chatauqua Press.

Edward Carpenter. England's Ideal, p. 13. London: Swan Sonnenschein, Lowery & Co.

1888

Richard Garnett. Life of Ralph Waldo Emerson (Great Writers Series), p. 157. London: Walter Scott.

Walter Besant. The Eulogy of Richard Jefferies, p. 221. London: Longmans, Green & Co.

H. S. Salt. Literary Sketches, p. 124. London: Swan Sonnenschein, Lowery & Co.

William Sharp. Encyclopedia Britannica. Ninth edition. London.

1889

Edward W. Emerson. Emerson in Concord. Index. Boston: Houghton, Mifflin and Co.

9   65

JOHN BURROUGHS. Indoor Studies, p. 1. Boston : Houghton, Mifflin and Co.

W. H. DIRCKS. A Week on the Concord and Merrimack Rivers. With a Preparatory Note, p. v. The Camelot Series. London : Walter Scott.

O. B. FROTHINGHAM. Cyclopædia of American Literature, vol. vi, p. 1000. New York: D. Appleton and Company.

PHILIP G. HUBERT, JR. Liberty and a Living, p. 171. New York: G. P. Putnam's Sons.

1890

DR. S. A. JONES. Thoreau: A Glimpse. Privately printed. Ann Arbor, Mich.

HAVELOCK ELLIS. The New Spirit, p. 90. London: George Bell & Sons.

CHARLES J. WOODBURY. Talks with Ralph Waldo Emerson, p. 69. London: Kegan Paul, Trench, Trübner & Co.

H. S. SALT. Anti-Slavery and Reform Papers, with an Introductory Note, p. 9. London: Swan Sonnenschein & Co.

HAMILTON WRIGHT MABIE. Our New England, p. 3. Boston: Roberts Brothers.

DR. S. A. JONES. Thoreau's Thoughts, p. 125. Boston: Houghton, Mifflin & Co.

1891

ARTHUR STEDMAN. A Library of American Literature, vol. xi, p. 594. New York: Charles L. Webster & Company.

P. ANDERSON GRAHAM. Nature in Books, etc., p. 66. London: Methuen & Co.

FRANK BOLLES. Land of the Lingering Snow, pp. 98, 102, 197. Boston: Houghton, Mifflin & Co.

1892

B. W. BALL. The Merrimack River, Hellenics and other Poems, p. 50. New York: G. P. Putnam's Sons.

GEORGE WILLIAM CURTIS. From the Easy Chair, p. 62. New York: Harper and Brothers.

1893

OSCAR L. TRIGGS. Browning and Whitman: a Study in Democracy. Numerous references to Thoreau. London: Swan Sonnenschein & Co.

W. H. HUDSON. Birds in a Village, pp. 153, 190. London: Chapman and Hall.

H. S. SALT. Richard Jefferies: a Study. Numerous references to Thoreau. London: Swan Sonnenschein & Co.

FRANCIS H. UNDERWOOD. Builders of American Literature, p. 213. Boston: Lee & Shepard.

Reviews, Criticisms, etc.
1849–1894

1849

A Week on the Concord and Merrimack Rivers.   George Ripley in the New York Tribune.

A Week on the Concord and Merrimack Rivers.   J. R. Lowell in the Massachusetts Quarterly Review, vol. iii, no. ix (December), p. 49.

A Week on the Concord and Merrimack Rivers.   The Athenæum.   London, October 27.

1854

Walden: or Life in the Woods.   A. P. Peabody in the North American Review, vol. lxxix, p. 536.

A Yankee Diogenes.   C. F. Briggs in Putnam's Magazine, vol. iv, p. 443.

1855

Thoreau and his Books.   Edwin Morton in the Harvard Magazine, vol. i, no. ii, p. 87.

A Rural Humbug.   Knickerbocker Magazine, vol. xlv, p. 235.

1857

An American Diogenes.   Chambers's Journal for November.

1862

THE FORRESTER. A. B. Alcott in the Atlantic Monthly, vol. ix, p. 443.

THOREAU. R. W. Emerson in the Atlantic Monthly, vol. x, p. 239.

REMINISCENCES OF THOREAU. Geo. W. Curtis in Harper's Monthly, vol. xxv, p. 279.

1863

THOREAU. D. A. Wasson in the Boston Commonwealth, vol. i, no. xxxiii.

THOREAU'S FLUTE. Louisa M. Alcott in the Atlantic Monthly, vol. xii, p. 280.

WALDEN. John A. Dorgan in the Boston Commonwealth, vol. i, no. lvi.

EXCURSIONS. The Boston Commonwealth, vol. ii, no. lx.

1864

AN AMERICAN ROUSSEAU. The Saturday Review, December 3.

THE MAINE WOODS. The Boston Commonwealth, vol. ii, no. xli.

1865

CAPE COD. The Boston Commonwealth, vol. iii, no. xxx.

WALDEN POND. The Boston Commonwealth, vol. iii, no. xlvii.

CAPE COD. T. W. Higginson in the Atlantic Monthly, vol. xiv, p. 386.

LETTERS TO VARIOUS PERSONS. T. W. Higginson in the Atlantic Monthly, vol. xvi, p. 504.

THOREAU. J. A. Weiss in the Christian Examiner, vol. lxxix, p. 96.

THOREAU. W. R. Alger in the Monthly Religious Magazine, vol. xxxv, p. 382.

THOREAU. Moncure D. Conway in Fraser's Magazine, vol. lxxiii, p. 447. Republished in Eclectic Magazine, vol. lxvii, p. 180, 1866, and in Every Saturday, vol. i, p. 622, 1866.

LETTERS TO VARIOUS PERSONS. J. R. Lowell in the North American Review, vol. ci, p. 597.

1869

FURTHER REMINISCENCES OF THOREAU. G. W. Curtis in Harper's Magazine, vol. xxxviii, p. 415.

1870

THOREAU. J. R. Lowell in Every Saturday, vol. x, p. 166.

1873

THOREAU. Dr. A. H. Japp in the British Quarterly, vol. lix, p. 189. Republished in Littell's Living Age, vol. cxx, p. 643, and in the Eclectic Magazine, vol. lxxxii, p. 305.

1874

HENRY THOREAU, THE POET-NATURALIST. British Quarterly, vol. lix, p. 181.

ELLERY CHANNING'S THOREAU. The Nation, January 8.

1875

CONCORD BOOKS. Miss H. R. Hudson in Harper's Magazine, vol. li, p. 18.

1877

THOREAU. M. Collins in Dublin University Magazine, vol. xc, p. 610.

STUDY OF THOREAU. T. Hughes in the Academy, November 17. Republished in the Eclectic Magazine, vol. li, p. 114.

1878

HENRY D. THOREAU AND NEW ENGLAND TRANSCENDENTALISM. J. V. O'Connor in the Catholic World, vol. xxvii, p. 289.

DAYS AND NIGHTS IN CONCORD. W. E. Channing in Scribner's Magazine, vol. xvi, p. 721.

1879

HENRY D. THOREAU: HIS CHARACTER AND OPINIONS. R. L. Stevenson in the Cornhill Magazine, vol. xli, p. 665. Reprinted in Littell's Living Age, vol. cxlvi, p. 179, and in the Eclectic Magazine, vol. xcv, p. 257, 1880.

1880

A NEW ESTIMATE OF HENRY D. THOREAU. W. D. Kennedy in the Penn Monthly, vol. ii, p. 794.

PHILOSOPHY AT CONCORD. The Nation, September 2.

HENRY D. THOREAU: SOME RECOLLECTIONS AND INCIDENTS CONCERNING HIM. Joseph Hosmer in the Concord Freeman, October.

1881

THOREAU'S PORTRAIT. By Himself. The Literary World, Boston, vol. xii, p. 116.

THOREAU'S WILDNESS. John Burroughs in the Critic, vol. i, p. 74.

THOREAU'S UNPUBLISHED POETRY. With a Portrait. F. B. Sanborn in the Critic, vol. i, p. 75.

HENRY DAVID THOREAU. With Portrait. F. B. Sanborn in the Harvard Register, vol. iii, p. 214.

PORTRAITS OF THOREAU WITH A BEARD. The Critic, vol. i, p. 95.

1882

HENRY D. THOREAU. John Burroughs in the Century, new series, vol. ii, p. 368.

SANBORN'S LIFE OF THOREAU. A. G. Sedgwick in the Nation, vol. xxxv, p. 34.

CONCORD AND THOREAU. The Literary World, Boston, vol. xiii, p. 227.

SANBORN'S LIFE OF THOREAU. George W. Curtis in Harper's Monthly, vol. lxv, p. 631.

EARLY SPRING IN MASSACHUSETTS. James Purves in the Academy, vol. ii, p. 271.

LIFE OF H. D. THOREAU. Theodore Watts in the Athenæum, October 28.

SANBORN'S LIFE OF THOREAU. T. A. Janvier in the American, vol. iv, p. 218.

1883

H. D. THOREAU. H. N. Powers in the Dial, Chicago, vol. iii, p. 70.

HENRY DAVID THOREAU. The Spectator, vol. lvi, p. 239.

HENRY THOREAU'S MOTHER. E. M. F. in the Boston Daily Advertiser, February 14.

1884

SUMMER: FROM THE JOURNAL OF HENRY D. THOREAU. The Nation, vol. xxxix, p. 9^e.

SUMMER: FROM THE JOURNAL OF HENRY D. THOREAU. Walter Lewin in the Academy, vol. xxvi, p. 193.

THOREAU IN SUMMER. The Literary World, Boston, vol. xv, p. 223.

1885

THOREAU'S POETRY. Joel Benton in Lippincott's Magazine, vol. xxxxvii, p. 491.

HENRY D. THOREAU. A. H. Japp in the Spectator, vol. lviii, p. 122.

THE DIAL. George W. Cooke in the Journal of Speculative Philosophy, vol. xix, p. 242.

1886

HENRY D. THOREAU. H. S. Salt in Temple Bar, vol. lxxviii, p. 369. Republished in the

Eclectic Magazine, vol. cviii, p. 369, 1887, and in the Critic, vol. ii, pp. 276, 289, 1887.

1887
HENRY DAVID THOREAU. With wood-engraving of the Ricketson medallion. A. H. Japp in the Welcome, November.

1888
SUNDAY AT CONCORD. Grant Allen in the Fortnightly Review, vol. xliii, p. 675.

HENRY D. THOREAU. F. H. Underwood in Good Words, vol. xxix, p. 445.

1889
HENRY D. THOREAU. John Burroughs in the Chautauquan, vol. ix, p. 530.

A WEEK ON THE CONCORD AND MERRIMACK RIVERS. Saturday Review, vol. lxviii, p. 195.

1890
THOREAU: A GLIMPSE. S. A. Jones in the Unitarian, vol. v, February, March, and April.

IN THOREAU'S COUNTRY. A. L. in the New York Evening Post, weekly, October 10.

THOREAU'S POETRY. H. S. Salt in the Art Review, London, vol. i, p. 153.

EMERSON'S TALKS WITH A COLLEGE BOY. C. J. Woodbury in the Century, vol. xxxix, p. 621.

THE LIFE OF THOREAU. The Standard, London, October 16.

THOREAU'S LIFE.   A. H. Japp in the Spectator, October 18.

THE LIFE OF HENRY DAVID THOREAU.   Walter Lewin in the Academy, October 25.

THOREAU.   The Speaker, London, November 8.

THE LIFE OF THOREAU.   W. H. Dircks in
the Newcastle Daily Leader, November 25.

HENRY DAVID THOREAU.   The Evening Post,
London, January 10.

THOREAU'S ANTI-SLAVERY AND REFORM PAPERS.
H. S. Salt in Lippincott's Magazine, August.

THOREAU.   Nature Notes.   J. L. Otter in the
Selborne Society's Journal, vol. i, p. 185.

LIFE OF H. D. THOREAU.   Animal World,
December.

EMERSON AND HIS FRIENDS.   F. B. Sanborn
in the New England Magazine, vol. iii, new series, p. 413.

1891

THOREAU'S GOSPEL OF SIMPLICITY.   H. S. Salt
in The Paternoster Review, March.

AN AFTERNOON IN THE UNIVERSITY LIBRARY.
S. A. Jones in the Inlander, vol. i, p. 150.

THOREAU AND HIS BIOGRAPHERS.   S. A. Jones
in Lippincott's Magazine, August.

TEN VOLUMES OF THOREAU.   Joshua W. Caldwill in the New Englander, vol. lv, p. 404.

1892

THOREAU'S INHERITANCE.   S. A. Jones in the Inlander, vol. iii, p. 199.

A FAITHFUL LOVER OF NATURE. W. Lincoln I. Adams in Frank Leslie's Popular Monthly, vol. xxxiii, p. 574.

AUTUMN: FROM THE JOURNAL OF HENRY D. THOREAU.   J. B. P. in the Vassar Miscellany, vol. xxii, p. 92.

1893

THOREAU. With Portrait. John Trevor in the Labour Prophet, vol. ii, p. 190.

THE RIVERSIDE THOREAU. Boston Herald, Monday, December 18.

1894

THOREAU AND HIS WORKS.   S. A. Jones in the Inlander, vol. iv. p. 234.

OF THE THOREAUS. Irving Allen in the Boston Daily Advertiser, Monday, April 23.

MR. SANBORN CORRECTS MR. ALLEN.   Boston Daily Advertiser, Wednesday, April 25.

MR. ALLEN'S RETORT COURTEOUS.   Boston Daily Advertiser, Thursday, May 3.

THE THOREAUS. Prof. E. J. Loomis in the Boston Daily Advertiser, Tuesday, May 8.

Years and Works

1840   The Dial.   Two contributions.

1841   The Dial.   Three contributions.

1842   The Dial.   Ten contributions.

1843   The Dial.   Ten contributions.
       Boston Miscellany.   One contribution.
       Democratic Review.   Two contributions.

1844   The Dial.   Six contributions.

1845   Graham's Magazine.   One contribution.
       The Liberator.   One contribution.
       The Union Magazine.   One contribution.

1849   A WEEK ON THE CONCORD AND MERRI-
       MACK RIVERS.
       Æsthetic Papers.   One contribution.

1853   Putnam's Magazine.   One contribution.

1854   WALDEN, OR LIFE IN THE WOODS.
       The Liberator.   One contribution.

1855   Putnam's Magazine.   One contribution.

1858   Atlantic Monthly.   One contribution.

1860   New York Tribune.   One contribution.
       The Liberator.   One contribution.
       Echoes of Harper's Ferry.   One contri-
       bution.

Posthumous Books and Papers

1862 Atlantic Monthly. Three contributions.

1863 EXCURSIONS.
Atlantic Monthly. Two contributions.
Boston Commonwealth. Seven contributions.

1864 THE MAINE WOODS.
CAPE COD.
Atlantic Monthly. Two contributions.

1865 LETTERS TO VARIOUS PERSONS.

1866 A YANKEE IN CANADA.

1878 Atlantic Monthly. Three contributions.

1881 EARLY SPRING IN MASSACHUSETTS: From the Journal of Henry D. Thoreau.

1884 SUMMER: From the Journal of Henry D. Thoreau.

1885 Atlantic Monthly. One contribution.

1888 WINTER: From the Journal of Henry D. Thoreau.

1892 AUTUMN: From the Journal of Henry D. Thoreau.
Atlantic Monthly. One contribution.

1893 MISCELLANIES. By Henry David Thoreau.
Atlantic Monthly. One contribution.

1894 FAMILIAR LETTERS.

Index of Writers

Adams, W. L. I., 76.
Alcott, A. B., 62, 63, 69.
Alcott, Louisa M., 69.
Alger, W. R., 61, 70.
Allen, Grant, 74.
Allen, Irving, 76.
Allibone, S. A., 62.

Ball, B. W., 67.
Benton, Joel, 73.
Besant, Walter, 65.
Blake, H. G. O., 50, 51, 52, 53.
Bliss, P. G., 62.
Bolles, Frank, 67.
Briggs, C. F., 68.
Burroughs, John, 63, 66, 72, 74.

Caldwill, Joshua W., 75.
Carpenter, Edward, 65.
Channing, W. E., 47, 48, 50, 58, 60, 61, 71.
Collins, M., 71.
Conway, M. D., 63, 70.
Cooke, G. W., 63, 73.
Curtis, Geo. W., 60, 67, 69, 70, 72.

Dircks, W. H., 44, 46, 49, 54, 64, 66, 75.
Dorgan, John A., 69.
Duyckinck, E. A. and G. L., 60.

Ellis, Havelock, 66.
Emerson, E. W., 65.
Emerson, Ralph Waldo, 47, 49, 53, 58, 61, 69.

Fields, James T., 62.
Flagg, Wilson, 62, 63.
Frothingham, O. B., 66.

Garnett, Richard, 64, 65.
Graham, P. Anderson, 67.
Griswold, R. W., 61.

Harris, Amanda B., 65.
Haskins, David G., 64.
Hawthorne, Julian, 64.
Hawthorne, Nathaniel, 61.
Higginson, T. W., 62, 70.
Holmes, O. W., 64.
Hosmer, Joseph, 72.

79

www.ingramcontent.com/pod-product-compliance
Lightning Source LLC
Chambersburg PA
CBHW030000030726
47499CB00008B/2830